# I Knew You Could Do It!

## Nancy Tillman

FEIWEL AND FRIENDS

NEW YORK

I knew you could do it!
I knew that you could!

Of everyone out there
I knew that *you* would.

And wow, holy cow, I am telling you, kid . . .
it wasn't easy, that thing that you did.

Don't think I don't know of the gumption
and grit and the backbone it took . . .
it took quite a bit!

But you dug in your heels
and you set your sights high
and you shook out your feathers
and made that thing fly!

You stared down
the dragon!

You made that ship sail!

And today you're the star of your own fairytale.

You did it!  You did it!

*Please say it out loud!*

You should be awfully,
awesomely proud.

I knew you could do it.
And you know what's sweet?

You're not even halfway up
victory street!

Oh, you'll be tumbled a battle or two . . . but you've got what it takes, you firecracker, you.

So when you get caught in the bramble and thicket, watch what you say to yourself—that's the ticket.

Don't get hung up in the should'ves and oughts and what ifs and could'ves and those thinky thoughts.

Remember the battles
you've already won.

Lean into the wind.

Put your brave boots on.

It won't be long till you're blazing
new trails and climbing your way
into new fairytales—

—swinging through stars as if there's nothing to it.

And guess what I'll say?

I knew you could do it!

Of all the things in the world most true,
I will always believe in you.

I have always loved fairytales, so my goal in this book was to create the feeling of one,
as well as to give a fond nod to some of the most beloved tales. While not every page has
a reference, many do! (Please see the list below.) I hope you and your children have fun
discovering them. And after you do, I hope you'll read them together.

**Snow White • Cinderella • Goldilocks and the Three Bears • The Three Little Pigs
The Wild Swans • The Lion and the Mouse • Sleeping Beauty • The Frog Prince • The Bremen Town Musicians
Little Red Riding Hood • The Goose That Laid the Golden Egg • Jack and the Beanstalk**

A Feiwel and Friends Book
An imprint of Macmillan Publishing Group, LLC
120 Broadway, New York, NY 10271

Our books may be purchased in bulk for promotional, educational, or business use. Please contact your local
bookseller or the Macmillan Corporate and Premium Sales Department at (800) 221-7945 ext. 5442 or by
email at MacmillanSpecialMarkets@macmillan.com.

Library of Congress Cataloging-in-Publication Data is available.

ISBN 978-1-250-11377-1

Feiwel and Friends logo designed by Filomena Tuosto

First edition, 2019

The artwork was created digitally using a variety of software painting programs on a Wacom tablet. Layers of
illustrative elements are first individually created, then merged to form a composite. At this point, texture
and mixed media (primarily chalk, watercolor, and pencil) are applied to complete each illustration.

1 3 5 7 9 10 8 6 4 2

mackids.com

*To my darling granddaughter, Cooper Jo,*
*a firecracker from day one.*

*—N.T.*

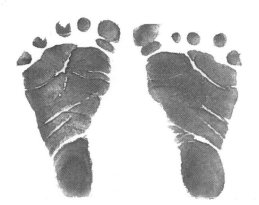

You are loved.